The

MAGIC
LAMP

Dreams of Our Age

The

MAGIC
LAMP

Dreams of Our Age

BEN
OKRI

with paintings by
ROSEMARY CLUNIE

APOLLO

an imprint of Head of Zeus

First published in the UK in 2017 by Apollo,
an imprint of Head of Zeus Ltd

Text copyright © Ben Okri
Paintings copyright © Rosemary Clunie

Artwork photography by Christine Soro, Goldmark Gallery.

The moral right of Ben Okri to be identified as the author
and Rosemary Clunie as the artist of this work has been
asserted in accordance with the Copyright,
Designs and Patents Act of 1988.

All rights reserved. No part of this publication may be
reproduced, stored in a retrieval system, or transmitted in any
form or by any means, electronic, mechanical, photocopying,
recording, or otherwise, without the prior permission of both
the copyright owner and the above publisher of this book.

9 7 5 3 1 2 4 6 8

A catalogue record for this book is available
from the British Library.

ISBN (HB) 9781786694508
ISBN (E) 9781786694492

Designed and typeset by Lindsay Nash
Printed and bound in Spain by Graficas Estella

Head of Zeus Ltd
First Floor East
5–8 Hardwick Street
London EC1R 4RG
WWW.HEADOFZEUS.COM

To my daughter, Mirabella Grace Okri.
May a wonderful light always guide you
on the unfolding road.
Ben Okri

❧

To my sister Margaret Wyatt and my brother Neil Clunie,
with love and gratitude.
Rosemary Clunie

Acknowledgements

With gratitude to Mike Goldmark, for his support;
To Ed Victor, for seeing the possibility.

'...and what is the use of a book,' thought Alice, 'without pictures or conversations?'

Alice's Adventures in Wonderland, LEWIS CARROLL

Contents

Introduction

Writing and painting come from the same place. But they have different axes. They come from the same dream and are soaked in the same atmosphere. Every line that wanders on a page, every word and colour, is saturated in the undercurrents of the world.

In this book the paintings came first. The stories came after each painting had been lived with for a long time. The stories do not illustrate the paintings. They reach to the world from which the paintings came, the under stream of our lives. There one dream shades into another in a vast sea of being that we all unknowingly share.

Paintings, like life, are a rich source of inspiration. But only those that give us access to aspects of ourselves that might not emerge otherwise. These are parallel glimpses into the underlying currents of our times.

The artist is a canvas through which the true colours of an

age seep out. The writer is a page on which the secret history of the times is written. Sometimes this history is oblique. Sometimes it is like a fable. And sometimes a colour or a form reveals that which we would rather not name. But artist and writer alike are prisms of the eternal and the contingent, the infinite and the political, myth as it is interpreted and history as it is lived.

Out of the same tube, we are squeezed; with the same pen, we are written. We think we write but the universe writes through us the veiled allegories of our age. Everything here reveals everything else that was in the air and that becomes more visible everyday. It becomes more visible and sometimes more alarming. Other times it is rich with the ongoing potentialities of liberation.

It is not against the blank canvas that the painter paints; it is not against the empty page that the writer writes. The canvas is peopled with infinite forms, but the painter chooses the true tangent between their own inner drama and the times in which they find themselves. The blank page is peopled with infinite stories, but the writer unconsciously chooses the best angle between their own inner conundrums and the invisible pressure of the times. That is all we can do. We geometricize our individual worlds and the atmospheric conditions that some call politics, others call history, but which are really the constantly changing faces of an enigmatic reality.

Just as no one knows what the period of time they are living through will ultimately mean, so we have no way of telling what the paintings and narratives in this book will eventually reveal.

Time is a riddle which the writer and artist interpret in their dreams. And their dreams are coded versions of all our dreams, given the tinge and temper of our mood and our spirit.

The spirit reads time through art. The spirit drinks the timeless through art. In that sense, writing is painting in the spirit, and painting is writing in colours and forms. They both point to the same mysterious allegory that is our lives. Seen as a prism, one face of it is politics, another face might be poetry, a third face might be war, a fourth face might be love, a fifth face might be art. But essentially the prism is refracting the same single unknowable reality in which we have our being.

Wander round this book as through the world laid out in the prism of words and colours, secret forms and hidden narratives. If we are going to change the world, we need to understand how it is made, and what dreams find concrete form in the forms of our times. It is with dreams that realities are made. We ought to work on the world as it is and on the dreams that daily become concrete in the hard stone and flowers of our times.

These stories and paintings were created in a spirit of playfulness. They were also made in a spirit of dream. Sometimes we had no other intention than to listen. Other times we had no other intention than to dream.

The spirit of playfulness yields lovely inspirations and hill-sides of red and yellow flowers. Playfulness is the dreamtime of the spirit. Light forms appear and dance across the stage. But behind them, sometimes faintly heard, mostly not heard at all, a somber music plays. It may be the music of mortality. It may be the music of transcendence.

Sometimes we are best when we play. Sometimes when we play mysterious things speak through us, like genies from a magic lamp.

Ben Okri

About the Paintings

These paintings were made by experimenting with colours and evanescent forms. The coloured textures came first, and suggested the forms and images. A narrative moment is crystallized into being from the inner world of the colours and their geometries.

All the paintings share the premise that we are an integral part of our landscape. The convention in painting has been to separate the two. But I believe things are interconnected, are linked, and interact with each other.

Rosemary Clunie

Prologue

I once found a lamp in a house I had just moved into. The lamp belonged to the old woman who formerly owned the house. She collected art objects from all over the world. After she died, her children left behind a lot of her possessions. I found the lamp with the sewing machine and the abstract paintings and bags of compost for the potted plants.

One evening, an artist friend and I talked about the mysterious source of paintings and stories. The lamp stood on the table in front of us. It reminded us of the famous lamp that had once sprouted a genie to the touch, a genie that performed all manner of magical operations.

Languidly, we wished that our lamp would perform a similar operation. Instead of a genie awoken from a millennial sleep we wanted the complete manifestation of paintings and stories, legends and poems. In short we asked for nothing less than the gift of perpetual inspiration. The idea was that we would conceive the wish for a tale, a painting, or a poem, and it would appear on the page or the canvas the following morning.

Lazily playing with this wish, we rubbed the lamp and went to bed. The next morning we saw the curious fulfilment of an idle fancy. First a painting appeared, and the morning after that the legend accompanying it wrote itself miraculously, in a clean handwritten script, on the pages of a black notebook.

We conceived the wish, played with the lamp, and at dawn the works appeared.

That is how the curious tales and images you have before you in this volume made their way into the world.

First their presence caused us alarm, then curiosity, then wonder, then finally a gratitude laced with a sense of vertigo. Had some genie really created these tales and images, and made them come alive at dawn? Or had we been our own unknowing amanuenses, working without knowing that we did?

At the beginning we accepted the gifts without question, submitting them to our daily sense of the marvellous. But then something peculiar caused us to doubt the beneficial nature of those gifts.

It is hard to write about it now without a sense of dread. I am writing with the double superstition that if I mention the terrible events the lamp gave rise to they will happen again.

Suffice it to say that these events seemed too close to one another to be mere coincidence.

It was then I glimpsed the strict economy of the universe, that even inspiration comes at a secret and unforeseen cost.

These disasters made us resolve to be more sparing in the use of the lamp. But as the events grew more serious, extending the danger to friends and loved ones, we placed very strict limits on what we demanded of the lamp.

It is now locked away in a silver trunk in a secret place deep in the earth. Only in the most pressing necessity will it be used in the future.

The price paid for such inspiration alarmed us. To keep what is left of a normal life we have placed on the lamp a seal of silence. We hope its genie will enjoy the bounty of its solitude.

We trust therefore that you appreciate what these stories and paintings have cost us. We offer you this volume in the hope that the strange gifts of the magic lamp may delight you on the obscure paths of life.

May you never wish for that which only genies can fulfil. Their gifts are always ambiguous.

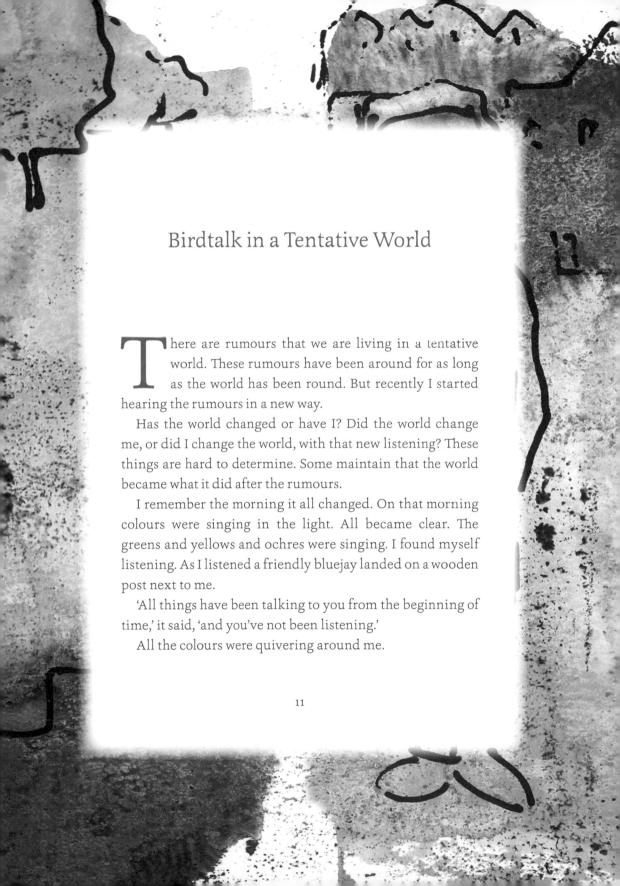

Birdtalk in a Tentative World

There are rumours that we are living in a tentative world. These rumours have been around for as long as the world has been round. But recently I started hearing the rumours in a new way.

Has the world changed or have I? Did the world change me, or did I change the world, with that new listening? These things are hard to determine. Some maintain that the world became what it did after the rumours.

I remember the morning it all changed. On that morning colours were singing in the light. All became clear. The greens and yellows and ochres were singing. I found myself listening. As I listened a friendly bluejay landed on a wooden post next to me.

'All things have been talking to you from the beginning of time,' it said, 'and you've not been listening.'

All the colours were quivering around me.

11

'You walk the face of the earth and do not notice that all things are dreams.'

From the earth a curious melody bloomed and turned into the form of trees.

'Every song I sing is a form of praise, and out of the praise things are made.'

I seemed to be breathing not air but the pure substance of things, an undevouring fire.

'What you call beauty is music in the soul.'

The more I breathed this fire, the more I felt the buildings around me hover. The world seemed in suspension in the fine spaces of the light.

'Everything wants to be raised, you know.'

It was a thought that passed through me with a mild seismic spasm. The greens and the ochres were silent. In their place the lilac sky was intoning a majestic syllable and it spread over the world an enveloping summer enchantment.

'All things have been talking to you from the beginning of time,' it said, 'and you've not been listening.'

'Even the colours change with your mood, it seems.'

I stood there, among the colours, as on a lost day of childhood when a wish that you had formed had acquired substance and appeared before you like a genie. I breathed gently and tried to keep the world from turning. I had to keep it still. The stillness was all.

'Did you know there are gaps in time that Heaven pours through?'

I shook my head.

'You are in one such gap now, my friend.'

With this the birdtalk came to an end. I stood there in the silence of the field. The bluejay craned its head towards me. I looked around. Had I been listening to the bird, or had the bird been listening to me, in this tentative world?

The Mystic Betrothal

They stand apart, waiting for the moment that will bring them together. He holds the last symbol of life. She stands protected against all that fire. They are the mysterious hope of the kingdom. It would take all the secret forces of the land to bring them together. It would take an act of magic beyond the madness of the times. They stand at the end of a secret tradition that has passed through Atlantis and the pyramids. The lost word quivers around them in the enchanted air. The world waits with the last dying flower for the difficult miracle.

Outside this ring of trees, they say the world is burning. In the evening, through the hyacinth leaves, we sometimes glimpse people falling from the high towers. They fall without a sound. Then, much later, across the waters, we hear the delayed cry of that fall.

Rumours come to us from beyond. Rumours of a church

in green flames, of wailing sirens beyond the tower blocks, of frozen music in desolate houses. Rumours of marauding bands of foxes who eat from the tables of abandoned homesteads, and who watch televisions that are never switched off.

Rats the size of dogs live in decaying maisonettes. The rats have eaten the foundations of the palaces. They can be seen in the square where the queen once waved to her sleepless subjects.

There is a steady murmur in the land beyond. Somewhere across the wasteland a lost symphony howls from a radio in a garbage can. A digital electronic heat has decomposed the colour of the clouds. The gibbering of the mad, the anxious and the disillusioned can be heard across the river.

Even atheists have lost their faith. Money brands the palms of those who hold it. Gold has lost its meaning. In the dry broadcasts of that electronic dawn we learn that the famous have lost their reason, the rich have lost their minds, and the beautiful have lost their glamour. The Government rules with the claws of crows. Only the indifferent get elected.

Outside this ring of trees, they say the world is burning.

But you are here now in this ring of trees. The turtle dove murmurs yellow melodies. Flute music waters the lavender and honeysuckle. The houses here are all symbols with spacious rooms in which the air is pure. The blue clouds create a reality that is like a dream. In this garden they stand and they wait. He holds the ankh like a weapon against fire. Her bridal dress is a panacea against all corruption. Her arms folded in benediction. Time is magical here.

The alchemical ceremony takes place under the aegis of the unseen masters. There are no witnesses, except our hopes. It is a mystic betrothal in an age of madness. The flower blooms again as the syllables renew the air. Something has changed in the heart of the fallen kingdom. The water tastes new in the rivers.

A Vanishing World

It is always there, round the turning. It is always there, round the turning of the trees. Round the turning of the trees, it is always there just vanishing.

There is blood in our eyes and rape in the scent of history. Women are bruised at night across the cities and are abducted in the dry North. Flowers are starved of pollen. There are oil spills in the guts of Dolphins and the fragrance of melted icecaps above the masts of polar ships.

But it is just beyond the turning. Beyond the turning of the page. Maybe the turning of the age. We who are here can't see it.

Then there comes one riding a horse with a golden saddle. His eyes are blue from a long Atlantean journey. In his saddle-pack a host of stories like genies from lost temples and forgotten pyramids. He comes while our world is on its last page.

The sycamore trees and the lavender bushes and the blue-bells sprinkled in the tall grass don't notice it. Don't notice the last page of our age. Nor does the mottled blue of the sky. Nor the yellow radiance of the sun in the body of the clouds. They don't notice it.

Just us who are here, breathing the electromagnetic glare, volcanic ash in our eyes. Our Vesuvius is not a rumble of earth and an embalming of cities. Our Vesuvius is in newsprint, in rumours and truth worse than rumours. In the dead eyes staring without wonder at the leaves.

But it is just beyond the turning. Beyond the turning of the page.

But it is always there round the turning. Round the turning whence he comes, leaning forward on his horse like a weary traveller from out of an old leather-bound tale. His robe yellow and brown, dust in his hair. Though we don't know it, for the air behind him is clearer than the air before him – he brings something we had dimly heard of in tales we learnt as children, when the waters were still innocent.

He brings with him – Oh, how can one say it without a flutter in the voice and a touch of the miraculous in the lift of one's heart – he brings with him just a hint of the vanishing world.

Yet all we see is a pale church lit by a purple sun.

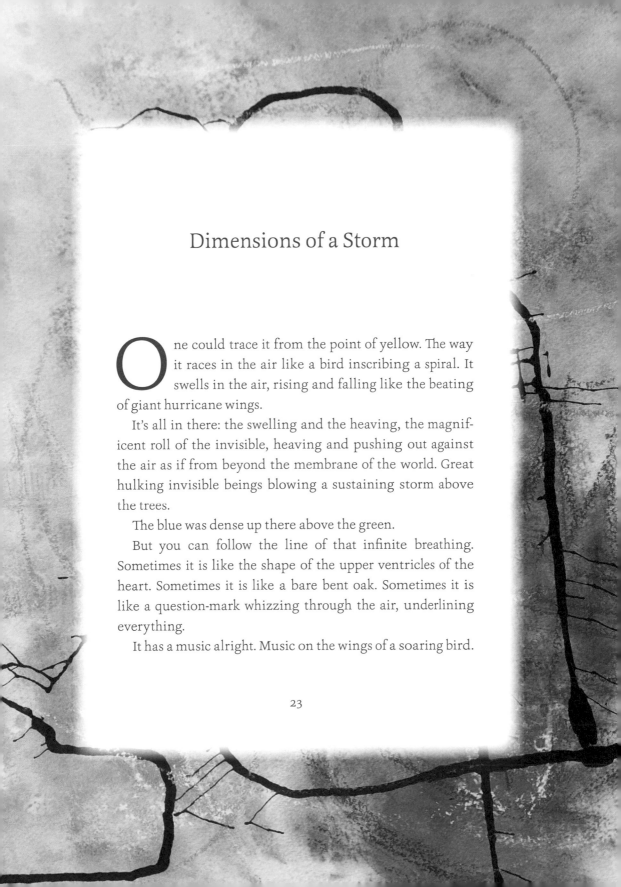

Dimensions of a Storm

One could trace it from the point of yellow. The way it races in the air like a bird inscribing a spiral. It swells in the air, rising and falling like the beating of giant hurricane wings.

It's all in there: the swelling and the heaving, the magnificent roll of the invisible, heaving and pushing out against the air as if from beyond the membrane of the world. Great hulking invisible beings blowing a sustaining storm above the trees.

The blue was dense up there above the green.

But you can follow the line of that infinite breathing. Sometimes it is like the shape of the upper ventricles of the heart. Sometimes it is like a bare bent oak. Sometimes it is like a question-mark whizzing through the air, underlining everything.

It has a music alright. Music on the wings of a soaring bird.

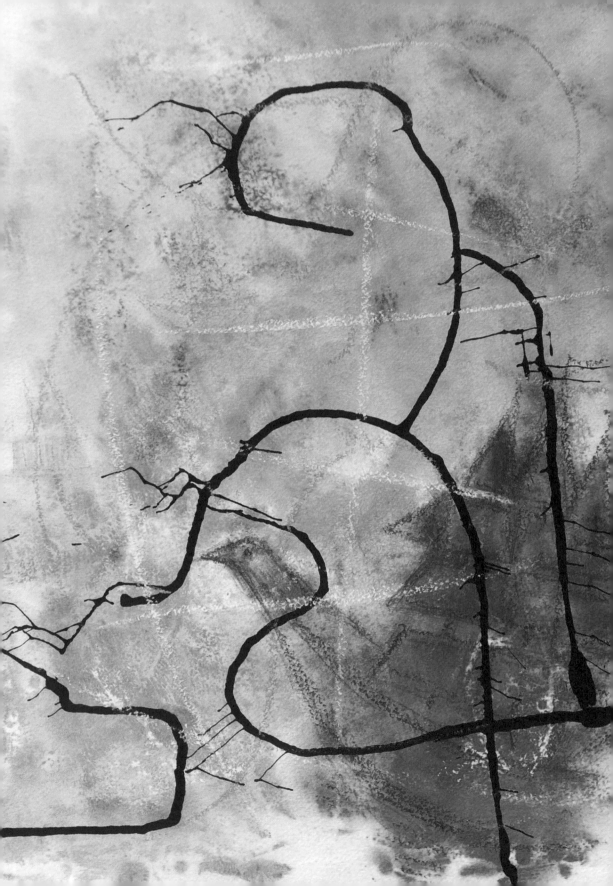

A bird with sails like a full-rigged ship on its
back. A red bird ascending in a blue world
barely seen. The breathing from beyond the
membrane obscuring all things.

The blue was dense
up there above
the green.

The treetops, all green, housing the
storm, are swaying as the leaves are shrieking
hallelujahs. Along the narrow road bordered by a
hedge, a tree is growing on a stone wall. The tree is now a
stump. But it is still growing. Its roots are in the stone, and the
stone is in the form.

The yellow is poised up there beside the blue. Just a
crouching, descending yellow. To see it is not to see it. All
one feels is the heaving and the treetops swaying and the
heart ascending. It takes some kind of stillness to feel the
dimensions of it all.

But you are a walking line on the landscape, whose meaning only those hidden eyes know.

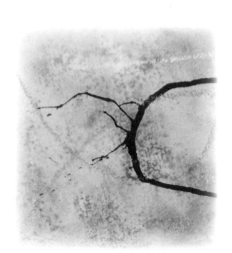

Artists of the Fading World

The colours left the world. They left like figures in a painting in the long glare of the tropical sun. The sun pours light on a world without light, investing objects with form. How odd that it should also drain objects of colour, like chlorophyll from Autumn's yellowing leaves.

The higher colours left first: the unappreciated violet, the misunderstood indigo, the neglected green, the polar blue, the ambiguous pink. Red seeped away ages ago with all that chaos. We lost orange in our solitudes.

The colours have mostly gone, but we are still here. Outlines in a fugitive world. We wander like drawings in a world of vanished chlorophyll.

Slowly all things concrete fade to insubstantiality. All that remain are lines. Where once there was architecture, now there is only the hint of their original drawings.

When the world fades, so do we. When we fade, so does the

world. We are fading into a dispassionate universal gold, the sunlight behind the glory of substantial things.

How odd to fade from light to quiet light. We retreat into it as into a reverse twilight, where everything is back to front. It seems the back is where things are more real. Luminous like a symphony from an unsuspected realm.

A sutra in light.

The colours have
mostly gone, but we are
still here. Outlines in
a fugitive world.

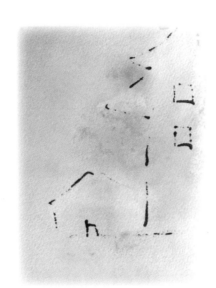

L'Époque Magique

Without knowing it we have crossed a magic line in time. We had been in the dark age of iron. It seemed to last forever.

Then one night the stars were brighter. A blue and orange fragrance floated in the air. It had a hint of saffron. Children in the poor district saw at dawn blinding flashes of a yellow angel's wings.

That morning we felt a tingling sensation in our feet. A mermaid with a piercing voice was singing in the far reaches of the Thames. A beggar was seen levitating at dusk on the outskirts of the city.

From the graveyard the skull of a dead poet was reciting forgotten terza rimas in reverse. An alchemist on a barge turned a dead pigeon into gold with a black powder. His incantations were impressive.

But in the street, one afternoon, the simple miracle took

place. A woman laced in blues and reds sprouted dark beautiful wings, under the astonished gaze of a gypsy child.

The age of iron is over. The age of magic has begun.

Unveil your eyes.

Unveil your eyes.

City of Enigmas

It grew its face over three thousand years. During that time, short in the mind of the moon, we had not noticed it growing.

The sea had its source in the rising sun, and the sun rose from the hills where the town began.

There is a legend that a child once rode his horse to the top of the last hill, and saw the river rising from the mouth of the rising sun. He was struck dumb by the sight, and didn't speak for eighty years. Then on his deathbed he made the cry that has now become a legend about the river and the sun. He was buried on the brow of the hill where the building grew for three thousand years and no one noticed.

The air here is translucent. Sometimes the light has the colour of jewels too long in the sun. The light from the river makes everything brighter. The houses are yellow. The roofs are blue. The windows are green. The lawns are golden and the porches are red. The gables are black. These are the colours we call them, but not the colours that they are.

The light from the river makes all things glow. There is a sparkle in simple things. Our boats are made of dreams.

In our farms we plant light. The wheat and the corn, the tomatoes and the roses and the beans grow from this light. Our harvests are rich with songs. Things grow silently here, but at night you can hear the moon waxing. It makes a low hum over the farms and the blue rooftops, and swells our bodies with fat dreams. Often we have to strap the children to the beds to stop them lifting into the sky.

The house that our forefathers and foremothers built on the hill was built with stones from the river. The women found the stones and washed them with their hands and their tears. They dried them on their breasts. Sometimes they nestled the stones in their beds and warmed them with their sleeping breath.

When the stones were too big, the women slept on them by the river. The men bore the stones at dawn before the river rose from the face of the sun.

The house was built slowly, as all true houses should be. A wall took a hundred years. The floor took two hundred. Each pillar took a hundred more. Three generations raised its roof. Its door made from an

Three thousand years and no one noticed the house was growing, because it grew from the silence of our lives.

36

oak felled by lightning took seventy years to shape. A long line of artisans honed the images on its face. Every child lent its life and its play to the house. The sun lent its humour. The air cleaned the face of our labours.

Three thousand years and no one noticed the house was growing, because it grew from the silence of our lives. Then we forgot the house that the sun had been building, forgot it in the times that came. The turning of the mills and the spreading roads took us away from the river.

Only now when we had long lost it, long forgotten that the river rose from the rising sun, do we see the picture that time has made. Only now do we notice the smile on the house, the smile on the face that has always been there.

The Domain of Uruk

No one knows when the domain of Uruk came into being. Some say it has always been here. It was here when the earth was young. Some claim that a voice from the sky reshaped the mountain into this brooding form, this giant head of an eagle.

It is a living form. At night the whole mountain, with its stone wings, soars into the night. The vast wings, spreading darkness over the realm, give the mountain a vertiginous lightness and monumentality. When it takes flight the land quivers. We have no idea where it goes. Wherever it goes, there we are. Whenever it returns, there we have always been.

There is a secret legend that the domain was shaped by a sorcerer artisan. A hundred thousand gnomes who were his slaves chiselled away at the rockface till this grim monolithic form was revealed. It is believed that the revealed form is the god that inspired the artisan in his atrocious labours. Since its

revelation it has haunted our lives with sinister laws and stern silent command.

There is nothing done or thought that is not witnessed by the all-seeing presence of the revealed form.

I am one of the watchers in the domain. I watch the moods of the land. I watch the moods of the people who live under the aegis of Uruk. From the unchanging countenance of the monumental form come the laws we live by. I study the laws. The generations come and go under the severe justice of the domain. I contemplate the generations.

Everything is seen by Uruk. There is nothing done or thought that is not witnessed by the all-seeing presence of the revealed form.

I am a watcher of the domain, and it is Uruk who watches through me.

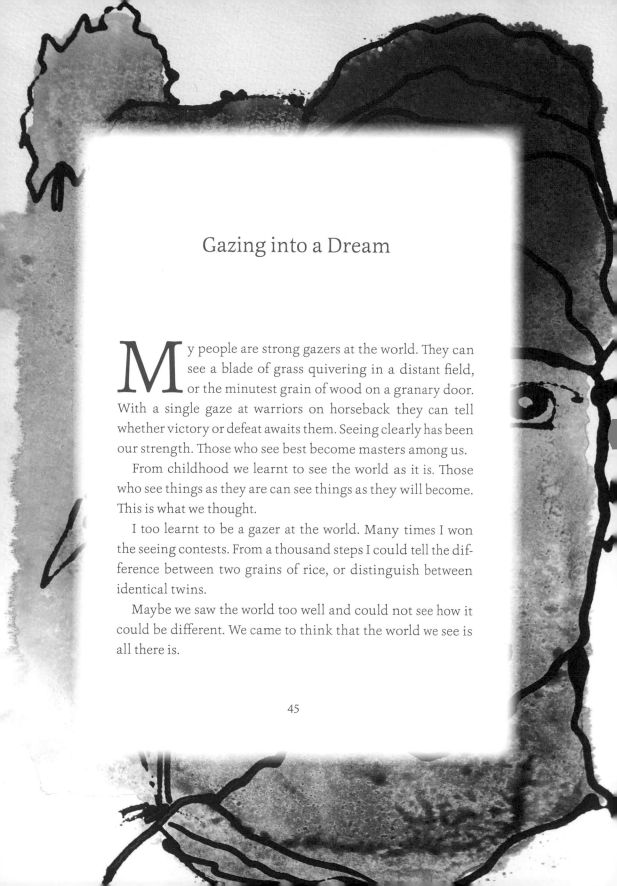

Gazing into a Dream

My people are strong gazers at the world. They can see a blade of grass quivering in a distant field, or the minutest grain of wood on a granary door. With a single gaze at warriors on horseback they can tell whether victory or defeat awaits them. Seeing clearly has been our strength. Those who see best become masters among us.

From childhood we learnt to see the world as it is. Those who see things as they are can see things as they will become. This is what we thought.

I too learnt to be a gazer at the world. Many times I won the seeing contests. From a thousand steps I could tell the difference between two grains of rice, or distinguish between identical twins.

Maybe we saw the world too well and could not see how it could be different. We came to think that the world we see is all there is.

But even with our clear seeing we began to be surprised by things that happened to us that our clear seeing could not foresee. Unexpected changes came upon us. The world eluded us in the new forms it took. People that we trusted betrayed us. The works of our hands no longer satisfied the depths of our souls. A new hunger came amongst us. We didn't know what we hungered for.

We who saw so clearly found that we had never really been seeing so well after all. The way we saw the world determined how the world revealed itself to us. The world had all along mirrored our seeing.

Then something changed our seeing. That changed the world we saw. I have no idea how it began.

One day I discovered that by gazing into the distance, without thought or focus, I could see things people only glimpsed in dreams. Often something happens in the world which I understand before it happens.

I became a gazer into distances. I peer into open spaces as if into another world. Then time dissolves. In the stillness of all things, I enter a place of simple happiness.

This is the place that my people have sought, a paradise among simple things. Sometimes the shape of events makes no sense till they hover on the rim of fulfilment.

I cannot tell what happens in this gazing *My happiest moments are spent gazing into a dream.*

place. But I have many beautiful experiences, many magical encounters. They seem to leave no impression on me except what is visible in my art.

When people ask where my ideas come from, I have no answers for them. I am of the tribe of artists. My happiest moments are spent gazing into a dream.

From the Magic Lamp

I was at a bazaar on a day when the light was blue. I travelled there through the medium of colour. Sometimes I sail there on the open carpet of a mood. It is a bazaar where only the things you don't need are conjured all around you.

To those with ordinary eyes, it appears empty: a blue space with a solitary mat on which someone had prayed. Many mistake it for the island of lost desires. Some take it for the ghost of marketplaces in the Orient, at the end of the long silk road.

Some I have known have found their way there on a flute melody. Some are drawn here by the slender music of the reed pipes. If you find your way here it will be because you have at last been overcome by those things which you sought but would not acknowledge.

I am drawn here by a lamp, which I saw once in a dream. It gave off a blue flame. When you spoke the right words to it, the

flame transformed into the perfect form of your most secret wish. The tragedy of life is that we often don't know what our most secret wishes are. If we knew what they were the lamp we seek would find us.

The bazaar today is empty and yet full of people searching for things with backward turned eyes. I see them looking at stalls and kiosks and tables piled high with lost treasures. They wander through the intersecting paths of the bazaar with their eyes facing backwards.

It seems everyone looks for something sinister and secret. One lady I saw sought hands as big as a wall. There are arcades for such things towering over the palm trees. One man I saw sought white shoes with which to walk the roads of the dead. But I sought a lamp in that empty bazaar where the spaces are blue. Then I saw him. He was sitting there with a turban like a quivering form in the air. He sat cross-legged. Lines of his spirit ran about him in a continuous zag of energy. About him there was nothing but the teeming emptiness of the Orient. With a shock I saw that his hand was a lamp. Out of the spout of the lamp stood a long flame of an unimaginable form.

I stand now in such a moment. The world pours through these blue empty spaces, dreamers seeking their most secret dreams.

Maybe the first moment of seeing that which you have

sought all your life is the most perfect of all. Like a dream, it stands before you. Everything before - the long roads, the failures, the lost wanderings – has led to this moment. All the moments after - the disillusion of dreams, the return of magic forms to their source - lead away from it.

I stand now in such a moment. The world pours through these blue empty spaces, dreamers seeking their most secret dreams.

Then I stepped out of my dream. I reached out and touched him, and found that he was not there. I found that the seated figure was unreal. The lamp too was unreal. It seemed that the form conjured by the lamp had dreamed the lamp and the figure into being. Maybe it had dreamed the bazaar too. It seems the dream has dreamed the dreamers.

I am here with the others. Maybe I am lucky to have sought the wrong thing, and to have found what makes things true.

Things Not There

His grin stretched across the landscape, intersecting the altar of the sleeping church. The house sloping on the hillside slid that bit more down towards the sea. The green was encroached upon by yellow.

A purple wind of trouble blew along the street. In the yellow house where the children hadn't eaten an argument started between the parents. The argument had sprung up from their bed.

His grin stretched across the landscape, and a bird flying past was stunned by a haze of blue. A flower behind the house thought again before it unfurled a bud. Somewhere in a barn troublesome dreams made the roosters tremble. Someone walking across the street was scorched by the distant glint of the celestial eye.

That day we were troubled by the memory of a yellow rose. The blossoms fell from the apple tree because he smiled. The

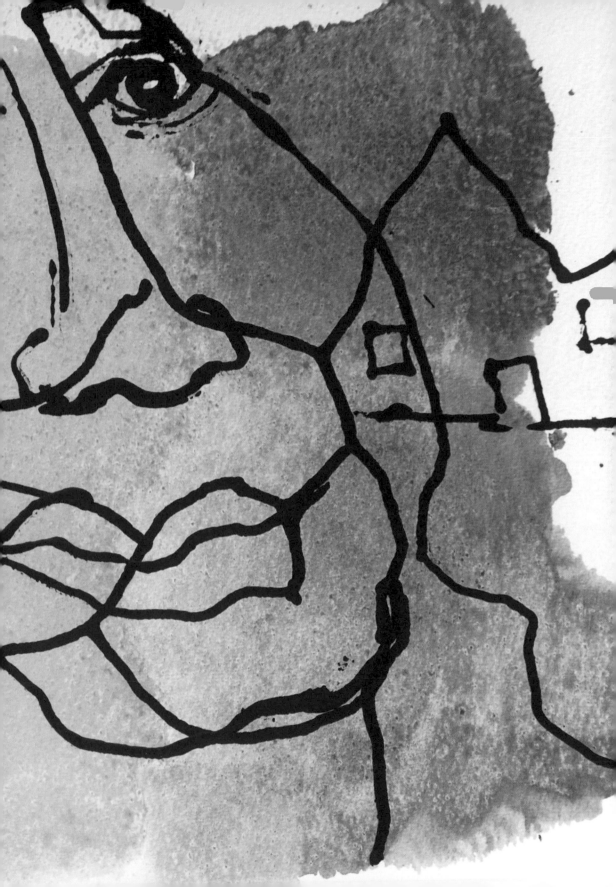

rim of the sky darkened a little. Somewhere a girl who could have been a poet started to weep. No one knows why.

His grin stretched the landscape, altering the spaces between the house and the church. But he was an outline in our minds, like the indeterminate silver of the horizon. Only the landscape saw him for what he was. The most potent things often appear not to be there. All we saw was a fading yellow mist in the air.

That day we were
troubled by the memory
of a yellow rose.

Return to the City of Dreams

He had left the city of dreams in his youth. It happened on a day when his parents told him it was time he realised who he was in the world. It was a morning of butterflies. The sun rose late on the green horizon of the river.

He had set off from the city of dreams with the bright stones of his father's words in his head, and the pearls his mother had made with her tears. His father had waved him off from the doorstep of their little house. The house overlooked the mountains and the distant waterfall.

His father was getting old now. The stick on which he leaned writhed with stories. As he left he was not sure he would see his father again and he looked back one last time. His father was bent in the doorway, a smile on his face whose meaning was too deep to understand at the time.

His mother walked him down the yellow path. It led

through the blue fields to the river. She too was getting on in years. But there was something almost eternal about the freshness of her eyes. She was silent the whole way. There was about her silence a wealth of parables which later he would unfold into his living experience.

At the edge of the river she said only one thing to him.

'My son,' she said, 'It is easy to leave, but hard to return. I pray that you return full of the meaning of the suffering of the world, and yet simple as the flower I am about to give you. The world will break you, tear you apart, rearrange you, disillusion you and maybe even destroy you. But if you keep this flower in your heart, you will return to the pure surprise of this dawn, to these gentle colours of our secret city.'

Then she did something strange. She plucked from the river-bank a blue flower. It was the only one that could be seen all around the river's edge. She pressed the flower into the middle of his forehead. To his astonishment, it disappeared into the thickness of his skull. A blue haze passed across his eyes.

Presences in the air, which he could not see, cheered his return to the city of dreams.

The sun rose, turning the greening of the horizon into a shimmering light on the river. A gentle breeze was blowing his yellow robe. He looked about him and was surprised to find that he was on a boat that was like a half moon. The ferryman was crouched on the prow. His mother was halfway down the yellow path. She had turned to look at him, but she did not wave. Then with the severity, which is also the tenderness of that land, she turned away and was soon lost amongst the yellow and blue.

The boat took him across the river, to the land beyond where dreams are forgotten. The land was called the real world. When he landed on its shore, the stones bruised his feet. When he looked back across the river, the city of dreams that had been his home was not there. Only a faint shimmer, a passing illusion maybe, lingered in the space where it used to be.

Many years later, when the world had beaten, re-arranged, and destroyed him, when he thought he had no home any-where in the world, when the hearts of men and women had proved cold to him, when there seemed nothing to live for, nothing to fight for, because all things in that world of the real turns to dust or to ash, when all this came to pass he set out to return to the city of dreams.

The canoe that bore him across was simple as a new moon. He stood straight, while his suffering steered the canoe across.

The city had changed. Gone were the blue fields and the yellow path and the huts built with storytelling hands. An enchanted metropolis rose beyond the face of the young bride of a moon. Everything was bright. Music rose from the flowers and the trees.

As he neared the shore, he hoped to see his mother there. He hoped that she would sense his return in the crushing of his hopes. But there was no one there. From afar he could see that his father's hut was a lost memory. He knew before he got to the shore that he was alone.

When he stepped on shore tears fell from his face. Where they landed a blue flower sprouted. He plucked the flower. At that same moment he felt in the air the inaudible music of a vast chorus of delight. He felt in that chorus not only the voices of his father and mother, but also of the illustrious ancestors and the ever-watchful masters. Presences in the air, which he could not see, cheered his return to the city of dreams. But what they truly celebrated was that he had not lost the blue flower in the furnace of the real world.

Life is a Street Corner

A face is where roads meet. One road cannot make a city. It takes many roads to make life a fiesta.

A face is where rivers meet. It is where times meet. Each person is a marketplace.

On days when there is a hint of a rainbow in all things, do you not sense that buildings that have sustained our gaze begin to look like us?

Through those invisible greens and purples in the air, we look upon some facade and see our faces there. Cities are portraits of our minds.

That portrait is best where a touch of silence surrounds the figure. On a building where three streets meet a delicate face is discerned. This face is made of all that dreaming, all that suffering. Beauty squeezed from time.

Life is a minaret. Life is a crowded square. A stock exchange. The winding shores of a river.

Life is also eloquent in the pastel of a street corner, where silence meets destiny.

*A face is where
rivers meet.*

The Blue Crusade

We made many discoveries in the unseen realm. One of these discoveries was the colour blue. We could travel in this colour. We could pass through a certain tone of blue into the world beyond thought, where gods dwell. We dreamed in blue. Some of us made magic carpets of blue on which we visited our friends in remote constellations.

Our sages made magic with blue. They conjured with it, invoked it, and created protective spells with its inner nature. Our best potions are made with sprinklings of blue enchantments.

We made realities with this mystic colour. We destroyed evils with its potent flame. In our ecstasies we went through portals of blue to the source of our highest joys. No darkness of mind but cannot be soothed and dissolved by its ministrations.

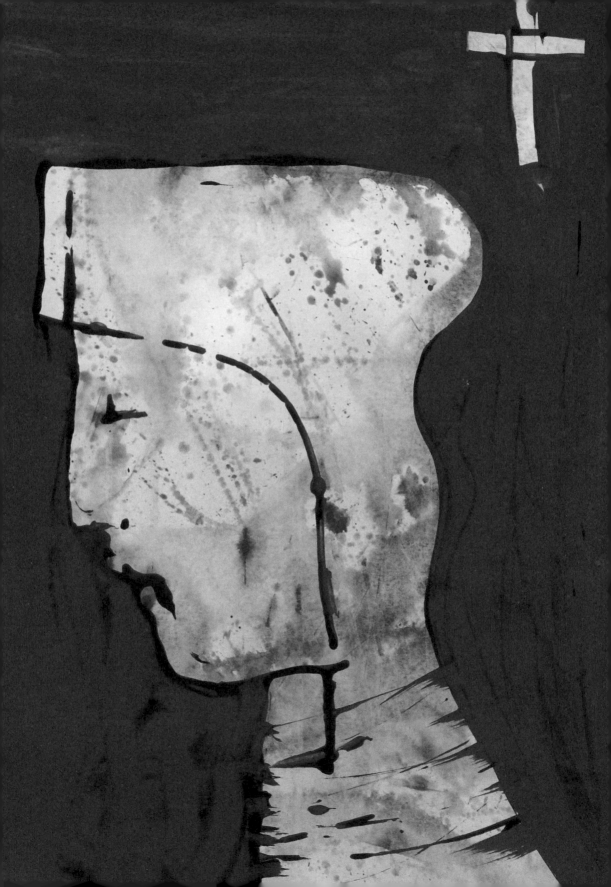

Then, over time, this blue wisdom was lost. We lost it as we grew more successful in the world. We lost it in the age of realism, as we became masters at manipulating the forces of nature and the power of the machine. We acquired more knowledge of the world and less knowledge of ourselves. We knew more, but somehow we knew less.

We became more powerful but lost the art of wonder-working. We lost the art and the magic of the beyond. It was only a matter of time before our power and our success would diminish. It would diminish and fade because of the lost art of blue.

Then, as if waking from a dream, a few of us realised that we could no longer travel on magic carpets of the mysterious hue to our friends and lovers on distant constellations. We realised we could no longer pass into the immeasurable world where the gods dwelt. We felt keenly our diminished mysteries. We sensed the hollow times that were already looming above us in our faded vitality, our creative impotence, and the neurosis that had crept unseen into the minds of our children.

The silent ones among us sought out the paths of the lost tradition. The listening ones among us left the cities and went deep into the forests and hills and sought out the forgotten mages. Through symbols and rituals, passing through death into new life, we re-learned fragments of the lost dream. Then we were charged with the noblest and most secret tasks. We were to take, to all corners of the world, the blue crusade. We were to awaken it in all those who secretly quivered to the music of the spheres.

Through the eyes of history this underground crusade had no apparent cause. But maybe, from the invisible world, the forgotten beauty of blue, missing our love of transcendent travel, took us up as a crusade. In this tentative world one can never be sure. The cause could well be the effect, and the effect the cause.

We acquired more
knowledge of the world and
less knowledge of ourselves.
We knew more, but somehow
we knew less.

Poet by the Sea

He emerged from the sea early in the afternoon, having spent the morning deciphering hieroglyphs. He had been contemplating the meaning of footsteps along the shore, and interpreting the cries circulating from the other side of the world.

The sea, in its obscure rage, had destroyed ancient temples and prosperous towns. Earthquakes had inscribed gaps in mountains and human destiny. The gossip of fishes had brought him news of imperfect revolutions in crescent lands.

Labouring among the symbols of alchemists, he had been aware of the murmurings of history. Late in the morning he had wandered among the seaflowers and the riverbed acacias. He had been charmed by the flight of the water swallows emigrating to temperate seas.

It had been a long morning. It had been a long morning of human history. From the moment when man, touched by

an obscure impulse, stood up on two legs, to the moment, a million years later, when he stood up in his mind. A long morning. Barely enough time to witness the growth of pyramids and the regret of nuclear realities. But long enough to have a conversation with those multicoloured fishes that swim in and out of dreams.

Late in the morning a message from his guide appeared among his poems. His guide sometimes appeared as a blue fire and sometimes as a golden wisp of incense smoke. This was the message:

'Time to leave the deep. Time to wander among the debris of human dreams.

Time to read the signature of the sublime in the fallen trees, the orphan's voices, and the songs of abducted women.

Time to rebloom the withered trees, without the supernatural.'

He finished his tea, put on a high-collared coat of fuchsia, and emerged into the early afternoon. Like a poem drifting in the wind, he merged with the blue doorways.

Only those who love the myrtle and the dove and the wand of Merlin saw the poet, wandering by the sea.

It had been a long morning.

*A faint troubled blush
rose deep within the Vine, and
made it tremble, as when
a fable of the wind turns
suddenly dark.*

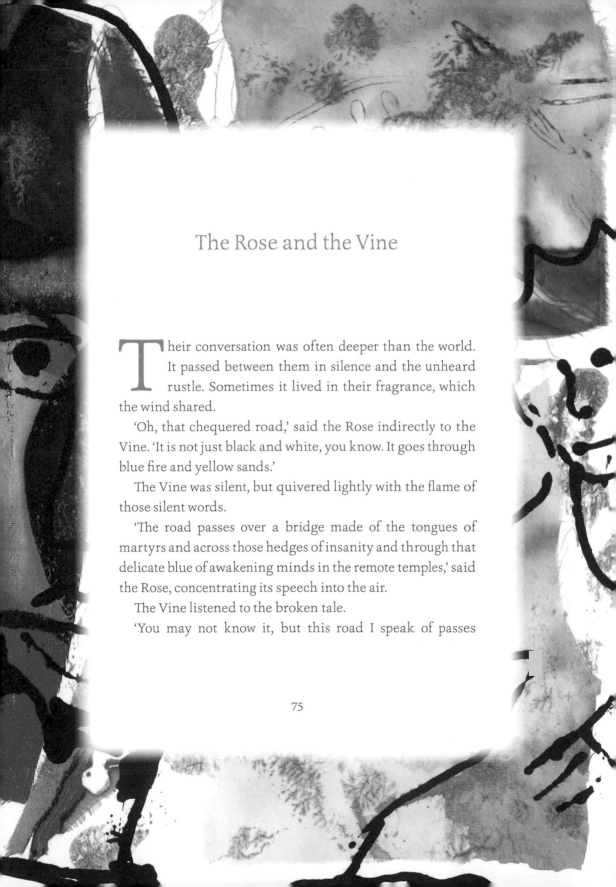

The Rose and the Vine

Their conversation was often deeper than the world. It passed between them in silence and the unheard rustle. Sometimes it lived in their fragrance, which the wind shared.

'Oh, that chequered road,' said the Rose indirectly to the Vine. 'It is not just black and white, you know. It goes through blue fire and yellow sands.'

The Vine was silent, but quivered lightly with the flame of those silent words.

'The road passes over a bridge made of the tongues of martyrs and across those hedges of insanity and through that delicate blue of awakening minds in the remote temples,' said the Rose, concentrating its speech into the air.

The Vine listened to the broken tale.

'You may not know it, but this road I speak of passes

through the dreams of gods and the screams of children. It beholds the slow rot of daily life.'

A faint troubled blush rose deep within the Vine, and made it tremble, as when a fable of the wind turns suddenly dark.

'Sometimes the road leaves the earth and ascends to the fiery moon, where it is repudiated by the stars,' said the Rose with the joy of its radiant mood.

The Vine sensed now the enigma of that mood and allowed itself to be shaken by its magic.

'You too have heard the obscure sounds the Sybils make that trouble our sleep with prophecies. The sounds come from the earth, and the earth is pregnant with dreams and night-mares. Sometimes flowers sprout from the blood and bones, and carpet the road with colours. Those who walk the road breathe the colours as hope.'

The Vine, full to its edge with the fable, replied:

'That is the road that flows in my veins. But with my grapes it is crushed into that liquid, touched with the gold of the stars, that makes men free.'

All around them was the many-coloured wind in the arbour, and the fable shared was their conversation with the sky.

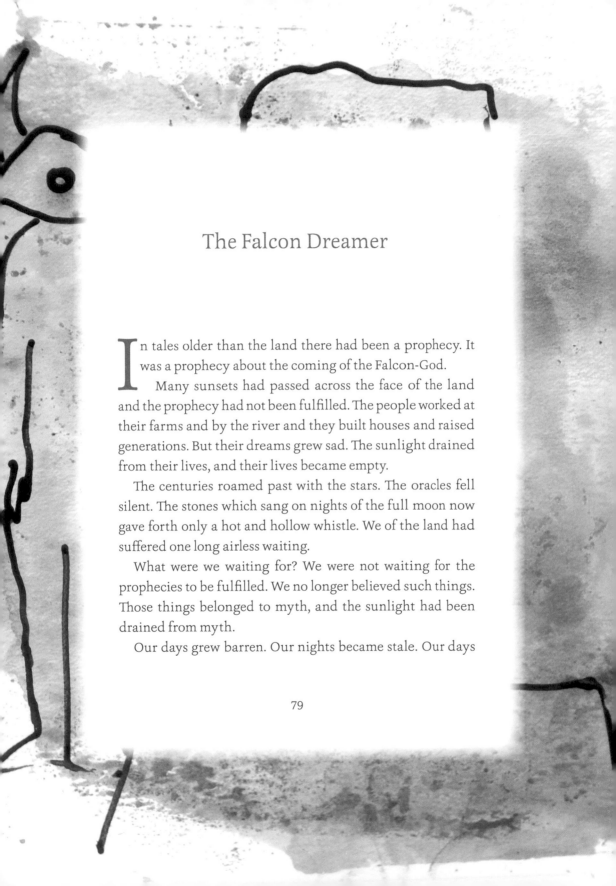

The Falcon Dreamer

In tales older than the land there had been a prophecy. It was a prophecy about the coming of the Falcon-God.

Many sunsets had passed across the face of the land and the prophecy had not been fulfilled. The people worked at their farms and by the river and they built houses and raised generations. But their dreams grew sad. The sunlight drained from their lives, and their lives became empty.

The centuries roamed past with the stars. The oracles fell silent. The stones which sang on nights of the full moon now gave forth only a hot and hollow whistle. We of the land had suffered one long airless waiting.

What were we waiting for? We were not waiting for the prophecies to be fulfilled. We no longer believed such things. Those things belonged to myth, and the sunlight had been drained from myth.

Our days grew barren. Our nights became stale. Our days

and our nights passed with undifferentiated steadiness. What did we have to live for? Nothing that we could remember. We just lived because the air sustained us, because some fragments of tales older than the land still whispered something to us. Whispered something we did not understand. In our not understanding there were occasional moments of beauty, but it was beauty as a promise of something unknown and maybe unknowable.

Then in that long barren century there came a man among us who learnt how to dream things into being. He learnt it from the myths we had discarded at the edge of the farms and along the broken shores of the river. He learnt it in the long silence and in the silent stones of the oracles. He learnt it from the old women who kept alive the last fires of the tales older than the land. The things he dreamt at first could not be seen by others.

One day, after we had been living a long time in fear and emptiness, the dreamer dreamt something he did not understand, something even he could not see.

Maybe a hundred years passed and no one saw it. No one knew it was there. But it was there all along. I have often wondered how long it takes a people to see that which has always been there. It is as if, over the millennia, we acquire the eyes to see that which we need to see.

It shone in majesty as though it had been there since the beginning of the world.

One morning, when the mist cleared from our souls, we saw something we had never seen before in front of the great pylon of the temple. It must have come among us during the long sleep of our minds. It must have grown out of our souls while we succumbed to darkness and doubt. It came out of those tales we forgot.

There in front of the great pylon was the quivering form of the Falcon-God. It shone in majesty as though it had been there since the beginning of the world.

No one knows what to make of it. Not even the high priests of the temple.

In one of the tales that treat of the prophecy as if it had already come to pass, there is the following enigma.

Had we dreamt the Falcon-god, or had the god dreamt us?

The Stoic's Season

It has been rather dry of late.
There's not much food on anyone's plate.
Even in the marketplace
Hunger speaks from every face.

Everywhere shops are closing down.
Even bankers wear a frown.
Misery lurks in every room.
In the papers there's economic doom.

The old have lost their creed.
The young are devoured by greed.
We're all drowning in fear.
This has been going on year after year.

But in a garden called Integrity
Dwell two wise souls, with dignity.
In lean years they kept faith and reason.
Lean years are the Stoic's season.

*Hunger speaks from
every face.*

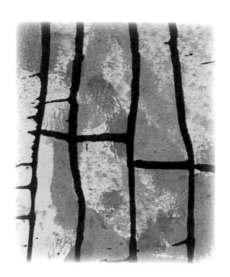

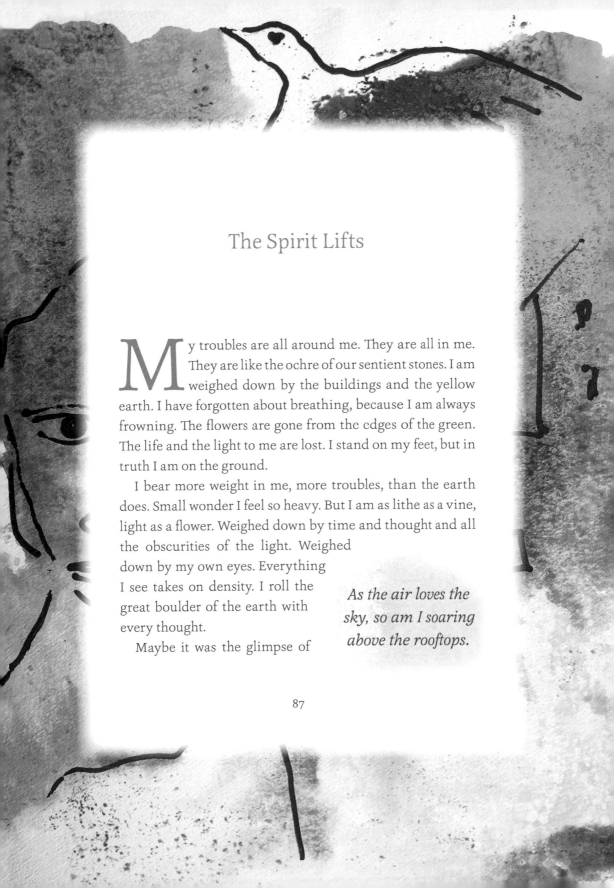

The Spirit Lifts

My troubles are all around me. They are all in me. They are like the ochre of our sentient stones. I am weighed down by the buildings and the yellow earth. I have forgotten about breathing, because I am always frowning. The flowers are gone from the edges of the green. The life and the light to me are lost. I stand on my feet, but in truth I am on the ground.

I bear more weight in me, more troubles, than the earth does. Small wonder I feel so heavy. But I am as lithe as a vine, light as a flower. Weighed down by time and thought and all the obscurities of the light. Weighed down by my own eyes. Everything I see takes on density. I roll the great boulder of the earth with every thought.

Maybe it was the glimpse of

As the air loves the sky, so am I soaring above the rooftops.

colour. Maybe it was an unexpected breath. Maybe something beyond the limit of the air touched my inward eye. But in the midst of my anguish, surrounded by the dark storm my own thoughts create like gods, I caught a glimpse of something within me, something formless. It was something that had an affinity with the air. Something made of an unseen light.

Suddenly I am in my true element. The spirit lifts. The mountain I carry within me is inexplicably dissolved, left behind.

My arms have turned to feathers, my upturned face acquires the pure shape of a beak.

As the air loves the sky, so am I soaring above the rooftops. My fears have been abandoned to the ochre of the earth. Upward lifts the spirit beyond the measure of the sky.

I have found my true form.

I am touched with something higher, something like the clear spaces, something like love.

*Then it seemed that something
was rising from the earth.*

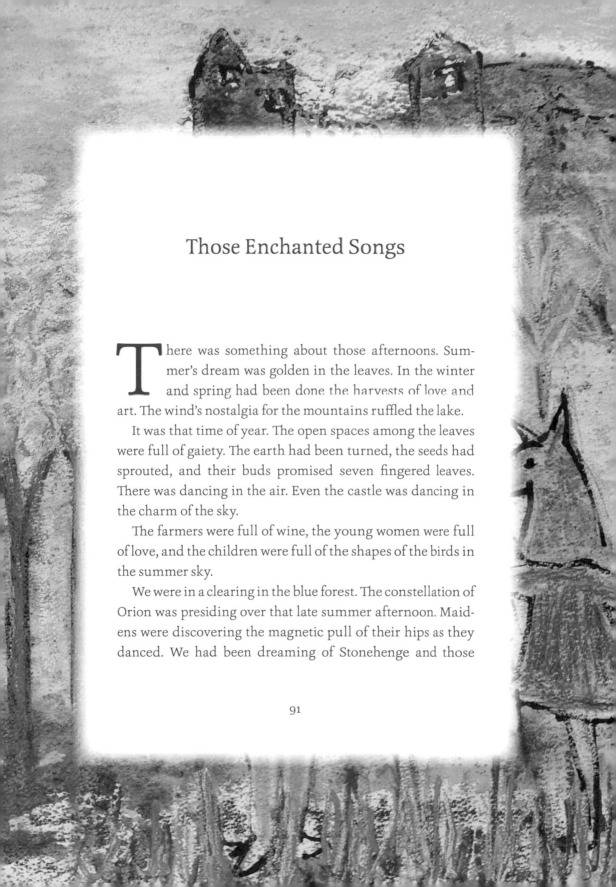

Those Enchanted Songs

There was something about those afternoons. Summer's dream was golden in the leaves. In the winter and spring had been done the harvests of love and art. The wind's nostalgia for the mountains ruffled the lake.

It was that time of year. The open spaces among the leaves were full of gaiety. The earth had been turned, the seeds had sprouted, and their buds promised seven fingered leaves. There was dancing in the air. Even the castle was dancing in the charm of the sky.

The farmers were full of wine, the young women were full of love, and the children were full of the shapes of the birds in the summer sky.

We were in a clearing in the blue forest. The constellation of Orion was presiding over that late summer afternoon. Maidens were discovering the magnetic pull of their hips as they danced. We had been dreaming of Stonehenge and those

ancient festivals in the ripe spaces. The air was tinged with those ancient presences. Out of the fluting call of the summer birds we almost expected their manifestation.

Then it seemed that something was rising from the earth. Some swelling in the air made me throw my hand up in exclamation. Then I noticed the one with the horse's head and boots of wolf's hide. He had a stone dagger in his belt. He had a horn for calling warriors out of the summer heat. He stood before us and made a gesture, compelling us to listen.

We listened hard. There must have been music out of which so much shone. The wind swelled the leaves and the trees seemed to rise. The bushes and the hidden bees in the flowers were full of the presence of the gods.

The afternoons were conjured from those enchanted songs, which no one heard.

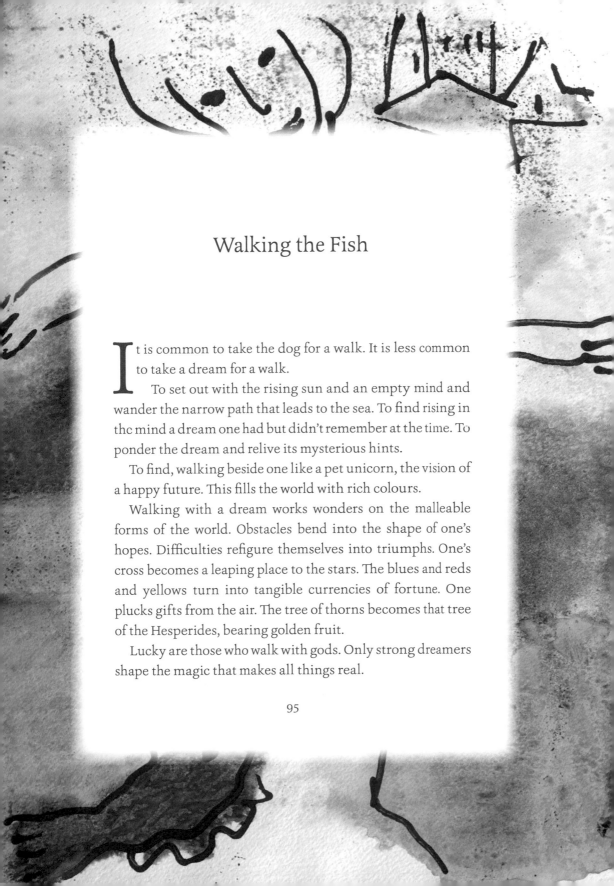

Walking the Fish

It is common to take the dog for a walk. It is less common to take a dream for a walk.

To set out with the rising sun and an empty mind and wander the narrow path that leads to the sea. To find rising in the mind a dream one had but didn't remember at the time. To ponder the dream and relive its mysterious hints.

To find, walking beside one like a pet unicorn, the vision of a happy future. This fills the world with rich colours.

Walking with a dream works wonders on the malleable forms of the world. Obstacles bend into the shape of one's hopes. Difficulties refigure themselves into triumphs. One's cross becomes a leaping place to the stars. The blues and reds and yellows turn into tangible currencies of fortune. One plucks gifts from the air. The tree of thorns becomes that tree of the Hesperides, bearing golden fruit.

Lucky are those who walk with gods. Only strong dreamers shape the magic that makes all things real.

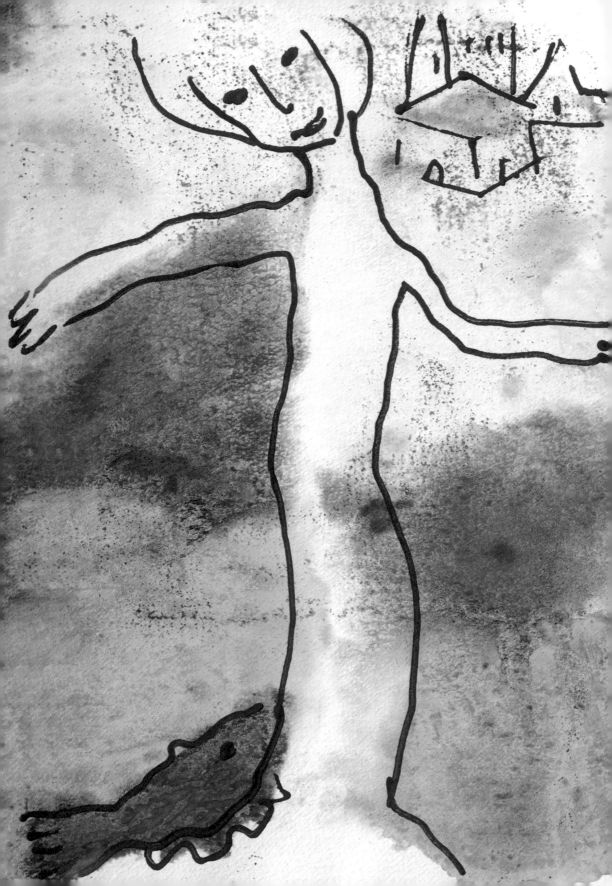

But how strange it is, on a morning when the air disperses colours like birds in flight, to find a woman wandering along the shore, walking her fish. She is curved like music from an Aeolian harp. The air bears the sea blues and the dazzling gold of her dress, in an aquamarine dream.

In truth she was not walking her fish. The fish was taking the lady for a walk. She was in a philosophical mood that morning. Not so the fish, who preferred the silence of colours.

'What are things made of?' asked the lady.

'Things are made of the way you see.'

'What is it that makes the way you see?'

'The way you are makes the way you see.'

'What makes the way you are?'

'Sometimes it is the way you feel.'

'And what makes how you feel?'

'The spirit,' said the fish, testily, 'whether it be open or closed, narrow or wide, whether it flows like the sea or is frozen like ice.'

'But what makes the spirit?'

'That's enough philosophy for a morning's walk,' said the fish.

She was in a philosophical mood that morning. Not so the fish, who preferred the silence of colours.

It might have happened in a parable. It might have happened in a missing gospel of women. The miracle then would not be the multiplication of loaves and fishes. The miracle would be our conversion into the mysteries of the sea.

Under the Sign

I stand high upon this crag and symbol, gazing down on the terrestrial world. Up here, beyond the brows of the sphinx, colours penetrate the sky. Far below, the world is made up of things, dunes, scorpions in the sand, and the shifting surface of the earth.

A man walks across the lonely immensity, going from nowhere to nowhere. Each step he takes is on burning sand. Fire in the soles of his feet, and fire on the scalp of his head. In the shade, resistance to green. Fire on the horizon.

But up here things resolve into laws. A man becomes a principle in eternity. The distant mountains like sleeping gods. Up here I see cycles, involutions, whirling planets like atoms in the cell of the universe.

I would rather be always poised in flight, with my wings touching the cool yellow heavens. It seems to me that one has a choice. One lives under a symbol, or one soars above

it. A man walks across an immensity towards death. He lives under a symbol. I am perched on the crown of the sphinx. I live above a symbol.

Below, the horizon is ringed with fire. Above, there is the limitless home beyond fire, where a grain of sand and a giant planet are the same.

A man walks across the heat of the desert, and yet the universe feels it.

Each step he takes is on burning sand. Fire in the soles of his feet, and fire on the scalp of his head.

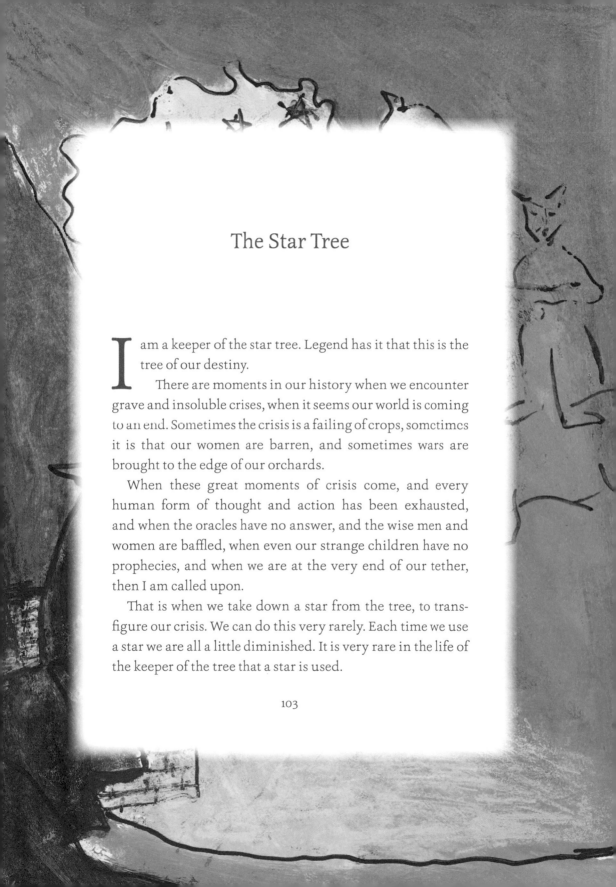

The Star Tree

I am a keeper of the star tree. Legend has it that this is the tree of our destiny.

There are moments in our history when we encounter grave and insoluble crises, when it seems our world is coming to an end. Sometimes the crisis is a failing of crops, sometimes it is that our women are barren, and sometimes wars are brought to the edge of our orchards.

When these great moments of crisis come, and every human form of thought and action has been exhausted, and when the oracles have no answer, and the wise men and women are baffled, when even our strange children have no prophecies, and when we are at the very end of our tether, then I am called upon.

That is when we take down a star from the tree, to transfigure our crisis. We can do this very rarely. Each time we use a star we are all a little diminished. It is very rare in the life of the keeper of the tree that a star is used.

My days are anxious and my nights are dark. I have night-mares. My nightmares are about the tree. Sometimes I dream that all the stars have fallen from the tree and burned holes in the earth and left our village covered with volcanic dust.

The tree makes me anxious. Its constant light is my unend-ing delirium. Its curious inward blaze crowns the air with a hallucinatory radiance. Sometimes out of its unnatural glow forms appear from other dimensions.

The space all around it is pure. It has an edge of madness. Its light is too hard for humans to bear. No one comes close to the tree, not by day and not by night. The night of the tree is brighter than sunlight.

The birds love its light. They fly all around it and disappear into its brightness. They never settle on the tree though. The cats bask in its glow, their eyes like spectral fires. Animals no one has ever seen before, nor will ever see again, sometimes leap from its light into our world, and disappear into the forests.

Sometimes the light of the tree is green at night. Sometimes it is bluish yellow. When the light touches my face I feel my head become distorted. My eyes then see things that leave me wrecked for weeks.

We are on the edge of a crisis now. I have to take down a star. When I step into the circle of its light I lose my iden-tity. I become as big and mindless as a giant. The people are watching in the darkness outside the circle of light. The pipes are playing and the drums sounding and the women praying. With my skin on fire and my hands raw, I wrench a blood-red star from a branch, and collapse into a millennial dream.

When all the stars are gone from the tree, what will happen? This is my nightmare. When all the stars are gone from the tree will it become the tree at the end of the world? Might the tree, devoid of light, then become a tree of evil? The land will have to learn to live without this light. We have to find more enduring illumination.

There are only so many stars on the tree.

Sometimes I dream that
all the stars have fallen from
the tree and burned holes in the
earth and left our village
covered with volcanic dust.

When We From an Angel Fell

Before the fall our wings were like eyes that saw the golden fruit in the tree of the upper world. There was an abundance of promise in all things. To think a thing was to have it realised. A desire was its instant fulfilment. A dream was its instant reality. There were no distances for the soul. The air was a pure kind of love, and to breathe was constant ecstasy.

Everything there held the memory of infinite worlds. In that world, I once held a feather that took me faster than the speed of thought to the edge of the eighth heaven. I held a pen there once and it folded into my hands the immeasurable, magical literature of an entire universe.

Oh, those books I read there that were life in the living. A single line of a poem once released into my veins a doomed enchanted history of Lemuria. An unfinished sentence was like water from the dark wells of Atlantis, and it filled my

heart with visions of successively extraordinary worlds. I held a brush there once and vast frescoes of walled cities in the seventh realm bloomed in my mind like technicolour mirages in a golden desert.

The spaces there house possibilities and impossibilities alike. I heard a note of music in that space and celestial symphonies lifted my wings into a strange blue air where I saw a multitudinous generation being born, living in ignorance, and expiring with a cry of gratitude.

But all that was when we were insiders in the unbounded temple of nothingness.

When we from an angel fell, time opened up beneath our feet. Love came rushing from the abyss. Nature snarled at us. That which sprang into our hands from a thought could only be hewn from the air with all the toil of our sinews. Meaning ran into every crevice and spilled out from the innocent surface of leaves.

Now we fall downwards, climbing up. We rush outwards, turning in.

The clouds above us reminded us in tattered fragments of that first space in memory. From the ever evolving seabed, a path unwound with our footsteps, tracing its way over the lands of the earth. What were dreams became storms. Before we had no need to breathe; now we have fire in our lungs. Before we saw without eyes; now with eyes we do not see.

Oh, but to discover that poignant woodsmoke of history, where bodies are growing from where bodies are burned, where flowers distill our putrid past into the fragrance of an unknown promise.

When we from an angel fell, all things were reversed, even hell. Now we fall downwards, climbing up. We rush outwards, turning in. The sea is mirrored in the sky. The substance that made all things is in our hands, like the lost word, which we have without knowing it. We forget how much we are at home.

When we from an angel fell, we became outsiders. We could become dancers in the infinite...

Prophecy

Once, when I was gazing into the air, a man with a crown, who was seated on a throne of gold, summoned me. He whispered things in my ears which became a green fire in my head. Sometimes out of this fire images take form.

I had always been gazing into realms of prophecy right in front of me and not known it. Sometimes I would stand in an open field, staring into nothing, and an event that would happen in ten years time would pass before my eyes.

In this way I have glimpsed lost wars, future births, the fall of empires, the rise of unknown powers, the changing fields, the dwindling river. I have witnessed lands devastated because the people brought to the surface that which should have been left in the deep. Sometimes I have seen

The grass stirs, and a heron considers the world with a question in the shape of its beak.

things which the ancient ones told me I could not have known, things that took place when the world was still forming. I have seen visions of our elders when they were boys and girls. I have glimpsed their dread initiations in the dark blue forest.

All this I have seen, just by gazing into the air. It is as if all time were here. It is as if everything is here, if we know how to see.

The grass stirs, and a heron considers the world with a question in the shape of its beak.

By gazing and not gazing into the infinite present, it seems all worlds are here.